WORDS

DARK TALES
DARKER POETRY
PAUL WHITE

PAUL WHITE

Copyright © 2017 Paul White

All rights reserved. This book or any portion thereof may not be reproduced or used in any manner whatsoever without the express written permission of the publisher except for the use of brief quotations in a book review.

TOAD

Toadpublishing@mail.com

DARK WORDS

We all have dark times in our lives; times when the clouds of uncertainty gather about us, when the shadows in our minds slam shut the doorway of hope.

These are times when the future looks bleak, when tomorrow is nothing more than a harbinger of anguish and our past lives a wasteland of futile labour.

Sitting in darkened rooms, listening to sad songs and reading dark words lends a little comfort to our souls as we contemplate the tattered remains of our world.

This book shares those days, the long cold nights of loneliness and apprehensive dread of what bleakness awaits us when the sun rises.

Like you, I have visited this world of soulless existence. It is where part of me shall always remain, huddled in the gloom, in corners of the deepest recesses of my mind.

Paul White

PAUL WHITE

CONTENTS

9 Bad Days

13 Late night

15 Razor

19 Eyes like ghosts

27 There is a storm coming

29 Such is life

33 Lies

35 Questions

37 My confession

41 Beyond night

43 Neat and Orderly

49 Today I cried

51 Bang Bang

55 The Kid

59 Rockabye baby

61 Regrets and no regrets

65 Jumping a boxcar

PAUL WHITE

73 Rejection

75 Empty spaces

77 Remorse

79 Wounds of Prayer

81 Clouds

87 Entry Denied

91 Fractured image

95 Lights out

97 The pebble bank

109 My special place

113 Six weeks

117 Leaving here

123 Overload

125 Roll of the dice

143 The Suitcase

149 Jack of hearts

153 When you go

155 Afterword

Dedication

Thanks to the Wicked Witch of the West for sending those Flying monkeys, Mark Anthony who let slip the Dogs of War and to you, the Straw Dog standing in their path.

I am behind you.... running away, fast

PAUL WHITE

BAD DAYS

All days are bad days.

The sun rises, it shines, it sets.

That is it.

Unless the clouds come.

The clouds which shadow my soul,

depressing and heavy, a blackness weighing down upon my spirit,

or what little remnant remains to keep my heart pumping,

to keep me unwillingly alive.

All days are bad days.

That is it.

Until it rains.

Until the sky weeps as I do;

a constant downpour of misery, soaking my being to the core, washing away all faith, until it is but a long-forgotten memory of submerged optimism, drowned with the loss of innocent youth.

All days are bad days.

That is it.

Lest the storm comes.

The storm I pray for during the dark nights.

Forty days and forty nights of pure vengeance, of retribution, of reprisal.

The dark thunder of vileness and forks of malicious lightning, sweeping away the evil intent of futile existence.

All days are bad days,

Unless death comes.

Until the grim reaper comes knocking on my door,

an offer to ferry me across the Styx, to Hades.

Blessed relief from Semele's infidelities.

All days are bad days.

PAUL WHITE

LATE NIGHT

Overlooking the city.

An eiderdown of crystal lights twinkling below,

twisting roads, snakes of amber slithering into infinity.

I am angry.

Marching up this hill, footstep after footstep, beating out emotion, tearing my sanity into raging shreds.

Staring over the city, gritted teeth and endless cigarettes,

Blue smoke snapped away by the wind.

Heavy breath, vapours of indecision and anguish.

Uncertainty and wavering anxiety, twisting knots in my stomach.

Riotous thoughts tumble untamed through my head, squealing like burning rubber.

Hands clasped, I squeeze my skull, nails piercing flesh, screaming out.

Falling to my knees, wet grass watered by the salty torrent of tears, the colourless blood of torment streaming down my cheeks unchecked.

I lay back, the ground as damp and cold as her heart.

Staring at the stars, pinpricks of hope as distant as my own.

The sky holds no solace, the air no comfort.

Life no future.

DARK WORDS

RAZOR

No double-edged flimsy foil,

no art knife or craft blade,

no snap-off tool.

I hold no faith with any of these.

Give me cold steel, hard and keen,

shining silver, bright and mirror clean,

weighty, unyielding, strong and thick.

This is my chosen tool.

Cutthroat, I say its name with pride.

Handle of timeworn ivory, crazed and polished smooth,

a mature blade, like sharply honed innocence.

I await its loyal service.

Now, my skin exposed, laid bare,

pulled taut, stretched out in anticipation,

awaiting the edge, the blade to come,

to feel its icy cold first touch.

My skin parts so silently, it softly separates

as the blade scores deep, slitting my flesh.

No blood, no pain comes forth at first.

I feel nothing but blessed release.

It looks like pink meat to me, deep pink.

One moment... count to three and watch,

as my crimson blood rises,

welling up and flowing out.

Again, the blade bites me, again and again.

It is what I deserve and that which I earned.

I am nothing but loathsome and hate.

I am below life's worth.

Yet razor is my friend, she comforts me,

erases my fears, my sorrow and grief.

Hallowed be the blade, thy edge of bright steel.

I wear the scars of our love.

PAUL WHITE

EYES LIKE A GHOST

I play with Blake.

Sometimes, when it is sunny we play in the garden. Sometimes we play catch, or we dig the dirt up and make mud pies and find worms and stuff.

My mummy and Blakes mummy sit at the garden table, drink wine and smoke and talk. They talk a lot.

Most times though and when it is raining, we have to play indoors. That is when we get the cars and soldiers and animals out of the toy box.

Sometimes the soldiers ride the animals and sometimes the animals drive the cars.

We play at the end of the room, under the big window.

My mummy says we have plenty of room here and Blakes mommy says it saves us getting under their feet. But I am too big to get under her feet. My head is as high as her waist, well nearly. Blake is a bit shorter than me, but not so much as he could be stepped on.

We are not allowed out of the big room… ever.

My mummy and Blakes mummy talk all the time. Even when they are not in the kitchen they sit at the dining table and talk. Sometimes they laugh. It makes me jump when mummy laughs because she is so loud it hurts my ears.

But they do not laugh very often.

Most times they are angry about something "I would not understand" and sometimes Blakes mummy cries. In fact, she cries a lot. My mummy cries when Blakes mummy cries.

They say rude words too. I pretend I do not hear them and make a growling noise as the sergeant falls off the hippopotamus and bangs his head on the truck.

"Shush, Crystal," my mommy says, "the kids will hear."

"Fuck the kids," Blakes mommy says glancing at us. "They're fine. "She lights another cigarette. 'Fags' she calls them.

My mommy pours more wine into their glasses.

I drank some once. The glass was on the table and I was thirsty, so I took a big gulp. It looked like Ribena but tasted horrible. I spat it out.

I don't know why my mummy drinks it. I once heard her say it was like piss. But she and Blakes mummy always have a bottle of wine when Blake and his mummy come.

They come to the house a lot.

Nearly every day now.

I am glad they come here because I do not like where Blake lives.

He lives very high up, near the sky.

To get to Blakes house you must stand in a silver box that smells like a toilet. My mummy says it is called a lift, but I know its name is Otis because it says so above the number 20. The number 20 is the one you have to push to get to Blakes house.

Once Otis did not get to Bakes house. I cried because I did not like it inside Otis and the smell made me sick. Mummy was cross because my being sick made her sick too. All her dress was covered in my sick and her sick and when the men opened the doors you could see they were not happy either because they looked at us funny.

Mummy washed me in Blakes house and I had to wear some of Blakes clothes. Blake laughed at me wearing boy's stuff. Mummy washed too and put on some of Blakes mommy's clothes. It was funny because we looked strange dressed like that.

The other reason I do not like to go to where Blake lives is the men. There are lots of men. They stand near where you get inside Otis and they say rude and nasty things about my mummy. Sometimes they grab her and sometimes they push her against the wall and put their hands inside her clothing. They say, "you like that, don't you?" and they say, "little slut" and other bad words I am not allowed to repeat.

Once a man took me from her and held a knife up saying he would pop my eyes out. I did not like that man and did not want him to pop my eyes out. The man-made mummy kneel on the floor in front of him and open her mouth. Blakes mummy came running up to us shouting and saying lots of rude words and screaming at the men who laughed and ran away. The man holding me dropped me and mummy had to take me to the hospital to see a doctor. He said I was lucky I had not broken my arm. But it hurt forever and I do not think that is lucky.

That is why I don't like going to Blakes house, even though you can see a long way from his windows. From his house, everything looks small and quiet, like a map.

But I think I am going to fall out of the window or the building will fall down and it's a long way down. It is scary and it is not nice.

So, I like that Blake comes to my house. None of the other mummies bring any children when they come. I don't think any of them have children.

Our house is a really big house, but I am only allowed in this room, the big room and the small room at the back, behind the kitchen, where mummy and I sleep. The rest is 'out-of-bounds' because it is where the other mummies work.

Aunty Caroline, who is the boss mummy, organises everybody. Every now and then she comes into the big room and calls my mummy away. "She will be back soon," Caroline says, "mummy has some work to do."

"Soon girl" she points at me. "Soon girl you'll have work to do too. I got some fellers wanting to get to know you while you're still young and fresh."

My mummy does not like Caroline when she says that. She shouts, "shut your fucking face." Caroline just laughs.

Even Blakes mummy must work when she comes here. Caroline shouts "Crystal, get your nigger arse out here girl, I got men waiting on you."

Caroline does not like Blakes mummy. She does not like Blake. "Little black bastard" she calls him. I don't know why, because Blake is not black, he is brown like me when I have been playing in the garden when it's sunny. But Blake is like that all the time.

Blakes mummy is a darker brown than Blake. But she is still not black. I think Aunty Caroline has something wrong with her eyes.

That's why I don't look at Caroline. She has nasty eyes, eyes like a ghost, a bad ghost.

PAUL WHITE

THERE IS A STORM COMING

The clouds gather again, like unwelcome guests.

Depressing in their greyness, dispiriting and dismal.

The musty scent of foreboding, heavy in the skies,

Carried on the shallow breeze of despair.

I sit barefoot upon the soil,

Watching the veil of depression muster overhead.

There is a storm coming, spiteful resentment and hate,

I have done nothing to deserve its fury.

Home is not a haven, nor my bed a shelter,

My door is no barrier for the wrath of lightning

That shall strike my flesh and let my blood.

My pain shall not fade with the parting of the clouds.

There is a storm coming my way.

So, I hold on to hope as feeble as the delicate flower grasped in my hands,

And I pray that someone without my storm

Can see the beauty of the petals and the hope within my heart.

SUCH IS LIFE

Life flows past, a river of time, ever-changing but constant.

Caught in its current as it pushes onwards, we cannot fight against it. All we can do is get by, survive until the next day.

I consider it a bonus to wake, to see the sun, hear the birds singing and to feel the wind on my skin once again.

I consider it magical to find friends along the way, as I am washed relentlessly downstream, towards the oceans of oblivion.

Such is life; my life anyway.

Perhaps, by some miracle or off-chance, I may have fallen into another river, a gentle stream or a babbling brook. Life may have been different.

Or maybe it will change or alter. Maybe a current will pull me to the bank, a gentle eddy swirl me to the shore or pour me into a lesser torrent.

Although I doubt it shall; however hard I may wish or pray.

The world is not like that.

In this world, you have little control over your existence.

Such is life. Your life.

We have what we are given, all else is but illusion.

Which is why it is important to grasp the simplest of moments, the slightest of chance, however small, however insignificant each may seem at the time.

We should have no regrets for reaching out, for caring, for showing love and affection.

Or for taking the same, accepting the comfort of another's arms. To be pulled close. To feel the warmth of soft tender flesh during those times our hearts and souls ache with longing and unfulfilled dreams.

Accept the little victories over uncontrolled chaos, over life's unjust consequence.
We have no knowledge of where this river of life will take us, how long we shall ride its currents or where our passage will end.
We know only our journey will be far too short.

The future is not our place of residence.
Ours is the journey.
Unpredictable, uncontrollable and arbitrarily erratic.
Such is life.

PAUL WHITE

LIES

The bitter steel screech of pain,

Cut my words, my lying tongue,

For those evil words, I loudly sang.

Crimson red, drips iron blood,

My phrases spoken, embittered lies,

Leaching salty tears from your eyes.

Silver scalpel, blade sharply honed,

Your heart I've crippled, broken,

My words should be never spoken.

Sticky wet pours to my chest,

I drop to my knees and I pray,

Will you please forgive me, I say?

You look, black in your eyes,

Dead to me and all my lying,

Rotting inside, already you're dying.

Now hollow space, I'm all alone

So, lift that scalpel and slice again,

Vindictive bitch, I need the pain.

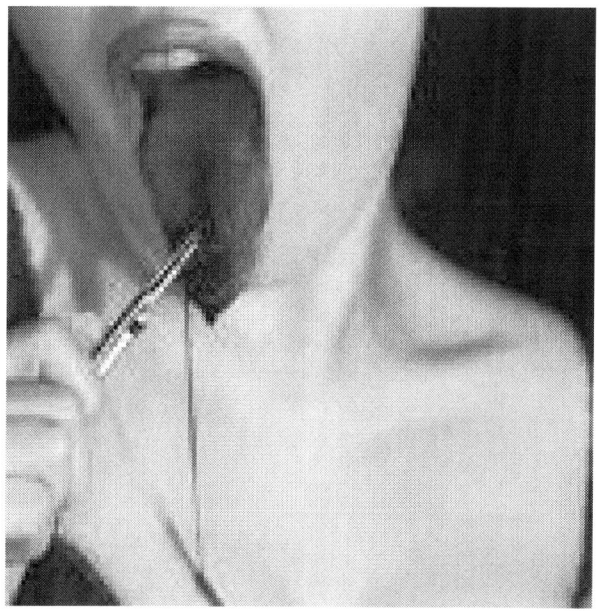

QUESTION

How many dark recesses do you have inside your head?

Those shadowy nooks that hide your innermost secrets and fears and regrets and feelings you once held for those whose names you will not even utter, anymore.

Where are the places those skeletons of your past reside?

Can you recall, can you remember?

Do you wish to summon their spirits once more?

Awaken the pain they bring,

Or to leave them forgotten, to wither away,

To decompose and putrefy, to fade

Until they are nothing more than the dust of forgotten memory blowing on the winds of possible future and hence dissipate into the fog of oblivion?

MY CONFESSION

I am guilty.

It is not your normal, regular, run-of-the-mill, kind of guilt.

This is far, far more… incomprehensible. One, which is as impossible to escape from, as it was to have been entrapped within.

You see, I loved him.

Once.

That once now seems so long ago it never truly belonged to me; which in all reality, I do not suppose it did.

All I had, as you may have now, is the belief life would keep its promise.

I never asked for anything more than was possible; I never asked for the fairy-tale 'happily-ever-after'.

I was not so foolish to think such things exist.

But, I did want it to last longer.

Yet still he has been taken from me, inexorably, imperceptibly, little by little, piece by piece; until there is nothing left of him, bar a thin parchment of skin hanging onto a frame of crumbling bones.

My love is in mourning for this body's previous tenant, the man who was part of me, of who I am, my husband, my lover, my best friend.

I fear each day that passes I should forget his voice, of how his hands once held me firm. I fear of losing the sound of his laughter, the remembrance of deeply breathing in his scent. These things are only with me now as the past, as memory.

I worry they too will be stolen from me, now someone else is living in his body.

I feel nothing for this interloper. I do not know him. I have never known him and have no wish to know him. That is why there is a distance between us, one which stretches much farther than the few inches apparent to the casual observer.

Yet there are social expectations which I must meet. So, I simply *'go through the motions'*, to satisfy the anticipations of others.

This is the guilt I carry, the burden which weighs heavily upon my soul, a guilt I have no way to assuage. This is my confession.

✶✶✶✶✶

Alzheimer's is devastating. Its reach affecting those about, family, friends and lovers. Alzheimer's brings with it an unwanted legacy of sadness, of depressive loss and senseless futility.

PAUL WHITE

BEYOND NIGHT

Today was just another day.

Another day; like all the rest which have slipped by

unnoticed and uncounted.

I prefer it that way.

Closing out the light with heavy drapes.

Sleeping.

Praying for the night, the darkness.

Stillness.

I sit in the dark. It is a comforting blankness.

Empty.

I rock, back and forth. Wishing the night would last,

Extend beyond.

Beyond life. My life.

PAUL WHITE

The Vodka burns. Harsh and bitter.

Yet it sustains the numbness,

Tolerates time and the waiting,

The waiting to die.

My hands were too wet, sweaty,

It was the fear. The fear of pain.

I could not clench the knife.

Shaking like the coward I am.

The pills made me sick.

Vomiting bitter bile,

Wrenching,

Before deaths cloak could fold around me.

So, I sit in comforting blankness,

Emotionlessness, detached.

I prefer it this way,

Seeking the darkness, the night

Beyond life, My life

NEAT AND ORDERLY

David surveyed the gardens from the large arched window of the library. This is where he liked to sit, particularly on a summer's morning. From this window, he could see the land beyond the gardens, past the stone wall boundaries.

To the right, which was in a westerly direction, the land gently dropped away, sloped down to the lake and eventually to the river beyond. The river divided this property from the next.

Looking out to the east was like looking at a different world. Here the gardens climbed upwards.

Many years ago, some clever Victorian gardeners, with the assistance of navvies and engineers, formed the higher levels into a series of terraces. As a finishing stroke of genius, they had created an escalier d'eau.

David liked to climb to the higher levels and sit near the top of the waterfall watching the flow fall away; a never-ending liquid slinky, a constant motion. It was relaxing, almost hypnotising. It was one of those things which made him feel calm and relaxed.

Past the high terrace lay the woods, some ancient oak and beech interspersed with plane and ash, other areas were coppices of hazelnut or planted with willow for basket making.

David had not ventured into the woodlands for quite some time. Not since the day he became lost in the oak forest. The dimming light, as evening approached, disoriented him and frightened him.

Luckily, Dr Griffiths heard his calls for help and came to his assistance, walking with him back to the house.

Looking straight on from the library window was to look along the driveway. It was a gravel avenue which stretched away into the distance before curving right, under the canopy of hornbeam. You could see no further than the corner from the library, although the drive carried on for another half a mile before it reached the main gateway.

It was five, or was it six years since he came through the gate? He could not remember exactly. David found that irritating. He likes to remember dates and times. They were important. They placed things in order.

Outside, beyond the gates, the world was hectic, irrational, confusing. It was one reason David had no wish to pass through the gateway again. He was happier here in the house, in his home.

Glancing momentarily at the longcase clock in the corner he noted the time. David's day was planned. It was the way he liked things. Neat and orderly.

At ten o'clock he would bathe, a hot bath and a good scrub down so he felt clean and fresh for the rest of the day. After his bath, he was due to walk in the gardens. Today he wanted to see how the green beans and tomatoes in the kitchen garden were progressing.

Mr Blanchard the undergardener, had shown David how to plant the beans earlier in the year and he was there again when Mr Blanchard planted out the young tomato plants. David was hoping the tomatoes were ripe enough to pluck and eat straight from the vine.

Once he finished inspecting the vegetables he would have lunch.

After eating, his plan was to sit on one of the garden benches and read, or maybe he would get the watercolours and paint for a while? That would be decided later.

David felt he was a very lucky man to be living in such a grand house. Nowadays most of the great estates were gone, or they were transformed into golfing hotels or themed pleasure parks. At least this house still included the tenanted farms, the paddocks, horses, stables and, of course, a full complement of staff.

That was a most important thing. There was no way on earth a house as large as this, a working estate, could survive without a full staff. It was a fact which had been raised on many occasions during various meetings.

David liked the meetings, they made the reasons clear, simplified things.

The door to the library opened. "I thought I would find you in here, David," said the nurse. "It's time for your morning bath".

David looked at the longcase clock. The nurse was five minutes early.

But then he thought, by the time they had unstrapped his straight-jacket and undressed him, his routine would be back on schedule.

It was the way David liked things.

Neat and orderly.

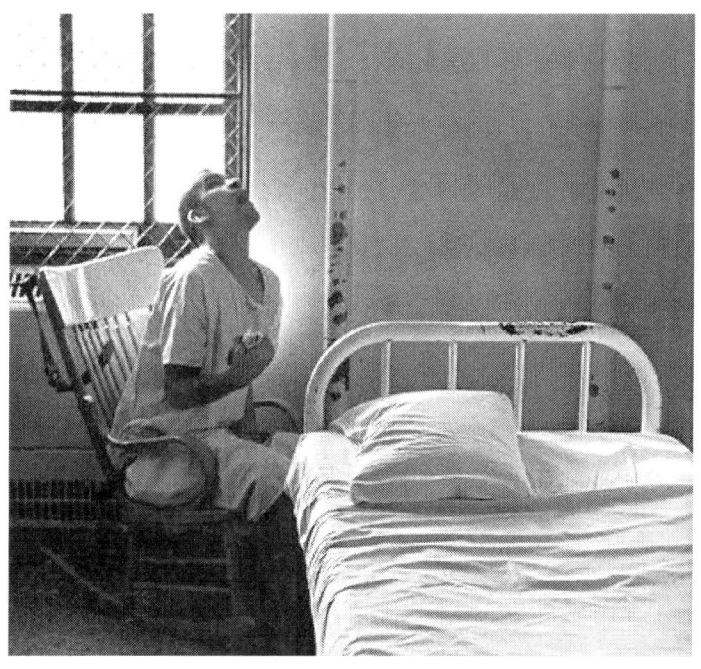

TODAY I CRIED

I do not know why, but today I cried,

It was just something from deep inside.

I was walking down a country lane,

When from within came forth great pain.

As the tears bust from my eyes,

I had to question my what's and whys.

I am not one normally touched by sorrow,

For I look ahead and see tomorrow.

But today, for no reason at all,

I knelt on the ground and began to ball.

I have not cried for years and years,

cause I bottle my worries, along with my fears.

Yet today. I completely lost all control,

Felt I had fallen into a big black hole.

My mind was empty, blank, a total daze,

My whole world swallowed in a misty haze.

Eventually, I climbed up, off the ground,

Just standing there, looking around.

Nothing had changed, it was all the same,

There was no eureka I could claim.

It came bursting out of my heart, out of my soul,

It was way beyond me, my personal control.

I do not know why, but today I cried,

It was just something felt deep inside.

BANG BANG

Sometimes they deserve it, don't you think?

To have their heads blown off,

To wipe that expression of smug satisfaction off their

faces,

Bang Bang.

Sometimes my fingers itch, you know the feeling?

To stick that barrel between their eyes,

To see their pupils widen in fear, shock and disbelief,

Bang Bang.

Sometimes I imagine the noise, the smell of cordite,

And their blood spraying over the wall,

Acrid and iron-rich rivulets of crimson,

Bang Bang.

Sometimes I wished I owned a gun. A big gun.

Big enough to rip their brains out,

Smash their skull like a funfair coconut,

Bang Bang.

Sometimes I want to have the courage, the strength,

To simply tell them to 'Fuck Off'.

Point my fingers at their head, drop my thumb and say,

Bang Bang.

Sometimes I want that gun, the Three Fifty Seven,

But I don't trust myself,

Not in their presence, not when they piss me off,

Bang Bang.

Sometimes I see myself pulling that trigger,

Feeling the kickback,

Watching the fragments of blood, brain and bone,

Bang Bang.

Because, sometimes they deserve it, don't you think?

To have their heads blown off,

To wipe that expression of smug satisfaction off their faces,

Bang Bang.

PAUL WHITE

THE KID

Sometimes I wonder what happened to that kid, the boy who took each day as it came, who sort of bumbled through life without much thought for the next day, let alone the next week, or even the future.

After all the future was a long way away. So far away, in fact, it was not worth thinking about, let alone worrying over.

What was worth thinking about was getting home from school, getting on his bicycle and going 'out' with his friends. Kicking a ball around, buying a cola, having a laugh.

That is what was important.

Not tomorrow, next week or next year.

While he never had his 'head in the clouds', he did not let the idiosyncrasies of the world interfere with his life. He took each day as it came and, being without expectation, made the best of every one of them when it arrived.

Life was simple, uncomplicated, without commitment, duty, obligation or liability.

I often wonder if that boy is still around, still here somewhere.

Up until a few years ago I often saw him, looking at me quizzically. Often it was just a glance.

Sometimes I would look back, staring into his eyes, examining his face.

He changed over the years, but he was still here, albeit dimmer and hazier than the last time I saw him.

But he was still here.

Recently, however, I have had trouble finding him. I have looked many times.

Once or twice, I thought I caught the slightest glimpse of him for an indistinct, unclear and faded fraction of a moment.

I am sure it was him. I am almost certain; but it was so very hard to tell, very hard to be absolutely definite he was still here somewhere.

The last time I looked was this morning.

I stared very, very hard into the mirror. I could not see the boy, not even a fragment of the inner child.

I could see nothing but a hollow space where he once lived.

I fear I have lost him forever.

PAUL WHITE

ROCKABYE BABY

Rockabye baby, broken and scarred.

Black rains a 'tumbling, falling hard,

Icy winds blowing, cutting deep,

Autumn leaves swirling into a heap,

She took the knife and held it high,

Cold steel pressed against her thigh

One more slice, deep into a vein,

Bleed out the fear, remorse and pain,

Closing her eyes, breathing out her last,

Sleep is coming, taking away her past,

Naked she lays, sprawled across the bed,

Hushabye baby, you're almost dead.

PAUL WHITE

REGRETS AND NO REGRETS

I have realised there is a difference between living happily ever after and just living after.

I may seem strong, but I am not. I am just like everyone else.

I too feel pain. I too hurt and I cry.

I will no longer be the one to destroy your hopes and dreams, to tread upon your visions. To hold you back, just by being here.

Never again.

I try to recall where it all went wrong, to remember exactly when things turned bad.

It has always been easier to say, *'fuck you'* than it has to face the facts, to listen.

I know that does not make it right, but we all protect ourselves the best way we know how. I have no idea how to erase the guilt.

I could sit here for days and talk about regrets and missed opportunities. I can list the million and one ways I have run away from myself.

I feel so screwed up, so completely twisted I spend most of my days locked away by myself and myself is not good company.

Not at all.

I do not come to this decision lightly. But now the time has come for me to move on.

That is it. That is me. I am leaving this world; hopefully to go to a better place.

I figure it is a good reason as any to die.

I would like to think you agree.

You see, when a person's usefulness is over when one is assured of an unavoidable and imminent death, it is the simplest of human rights to choose a quick and easy death in place of a slow and horrible one.

Isn't it?

I have regrets about my life, about living, yet I have no regrets about dying.

None at all.

PAUL WHITE

JUMPING A BOXCAR

Sunset.

The last train.

I was waiting by the rails, backpack on the ground, beside my feet.

My backpack was full. Everything I owned was crammed in there. Clothes, razor, soap, two towels, one face flannel, and three books.

That was it. That was the total of my life.

At least regarding material things.

You see, as I stood by the tracks waiting to jump a boxcar to wherever that train was going, I was carrying a far heavier burden than the contents of my backpack.

She had told me everything would be alright, things have a way of working themselves out.

But it takes time and I knew I had taken enough of her time already.

Three years.

Well, two years, seven months, three days and twenty-two hours to be precise. During which time I had broken almost every promise I ever made to her and that was unfair.

I promised I would look after her, get a good job, earn a decent income, buy her gifts, chocolates and flowers.

I promised we would have our own place, a nice car. I said I would make her happy, that we would be happy.

I said I would never leave.

They were all lies.

I was being honest when I spoke those words, but life has a way of making you into a liar.

Life has ways of sneaking up on you and driving a knife between your shoulder blades before twisting it back and forth.

Life is adept at pulling the rug from under your feet and viciously kicking you in the head as you lay screaming on the floor.

Yeah, life can be a bitch.

But there was one thing that bitch was not going to take from me and that was my main promise, my first promise. Life was not going to steal that from me.

Which is why I am here, by the rails, waiting for the train.

I took a last deep toke on the cigarette, holding it up before my face and exhaling, blowing the smoke from my lungs in a steady stream which made the ash glow bright red, like the setting sun.

Like a bleeding heart.

Like a weeping broken heart torn to shreds.

In that moment, for a millisecond I thought about going back to her, so I did not break another promise.

I will never hurt you.

Because I know when she wakes and finds I am gone, it will hurt her.

So, I lie once again.

I can see the train now, its lights blazing as it rattles towards me, guided by those unfeeling cold steel rails.

I wish I was as cold.

I wish I could not feel.

But I do.

I recall how warm she felt as I held her close to me, hugging her tight as I made the first promise.

I shall always love you.

I will always love her.

Life will not take that from me.

Only the grim reaper can claim that.

Only death can take it from me

Until then, I shall keep my first promise safely locked away in the comfort of my soul.

I reach down and lift the backpack onto my shoulder.

The train begins to pass.

I run alongside, grab hold, scramble on-board.

This, I realise is not a new journey, just a continuation.

She was just an unscheduled stop.

When I left, when I crept out of the room like a thief in the night, she was fast asleep. Hair splayed across the pillows. One leg poking out from under the rumpled sheet.

Rumpled from our lovemaking.

Our last loving.

I was a thief stealing away with her hopes and dreams of the future, our future. Leaving behind a void, a hollow I know she will never be able to completely fill.

I have left her with uncertainty, anxiety, the doubt of why.

Why I left.

Why I never told her

Why I did not leave a letter

A note.

I huddle into the darkest shadows of the corner of the empty boxcar. Like the place in my mind where I shall hold my memories of her. Not to be forgotten, but never to be revealed.

I justify everything to myself.

I am not a good man.

I could not find steady employment. I could not find work that paid enough to buy food for her, let alone flowers or chocolates.

I could never keep regular rental payments, so our own home was always just a dream.

If I was careful I had enough money for bus fare, but never enough to buy a car.

But I was rarely careful.

So, I walked a lot.

I am not a good man.

Not good enough for her.

Nowhere near good enough for her. I was just a weight, a heavy weight dragging her down into the gloom of hardship and depression.

Pulling her lower, to the gutter, to the sewers of my futile existence.

I want more for her.

I want her to be happy, to smile again and to dance with lightness and laughter.

I want her to see the sunlight of possibility once more.

I want her to have back all the things I have drained from her life over the last two years, seven months, three days and twenty-two hours.

You see, as I stood by those tracks, waiting to jump a boxcar to wherever that train was going, I was carrying a far heavier burden than the contents of my backpack.

REJECTION

The bleached white bones of desertion lay scattered on the charred earth of dispossession, as the last droplets of rational purpose are sucked into the dry ashes of dissolution, like the crimson seeping of let blood.

Cold shivers rack my body, my spine freezes with the icy blast of spiteful contempt blowing across the barren landscape of callous delusion.

What future lies for those of blind heart and pitiless soul, as bleak winters of dearth curl down upon us from clouded grey skies of resentful departure?

I ache with the pain of dejection. My breath rasps sore in narrowed throat, heart clambers against ribs of bruised ego, while salted tears flow on pale cheeks blushed with rubicund hue.

Crumbled down, a heap of curled sorrow hiding in dark corners of despair. Head bent, cradled on and folded arms, I weep away the hours of night.

Day brings only remorse. A scornful light, teasing of pleasure lost, love waned, lust disintegrated. Now only cold cinders of passion lay upon the white sheets where fervent delight and carnal hunger once entwined.

Loves heart does not bleed. Grief has already sucked it dry, a vampiric leaching, leading to an empty life hollow of being.

Welcome the hours of solitude. Welcome the silence of darkness. For in these I see no tears, I feel no pain. I feel nothing.

I do not think; therefore I am not.

DARK WORDS

PAUL WHITE

EMPTY SPACES

Nothing is okay, at least to me.

Hollowness, empty space, that's fine.

I can understand that,

I can cope with that.

It is when those spaces are not empty,

When there is a shadow,

A resonance, a trace.

I can't manage that.

When I turn my head and you're not there,

Or I start to speak to that vacant chair.

The fleeting glimpse from the corner of my eye,

A momentary timbre, a residual remnant.

Entering a room to see your presence fade,

A suggestion of where you once stood.

Or reaching out to an unused pillow,

Touching the ghost of your soft skin.

Sometimes I feel you touching me,

The gentle caress of your fingers.

Before I open my eyes, before I realise you are gone.

I hate that.

Occasionally I hear your voice, hear you calling my name,

Soft echoes of melody floating within my memory.

I can't handle that.

So, nothing is okay, at least to me.

Hollowness and empty spaces,

I can cope with those.

Just.

REMORSE

Winters words blew forth betwixt icicle teeth,

Stinging whirlwinds of callous disdain,

Born of cold anger and clenched jaw,

Pursed lips snarling like wind whipping boughs.

Looking back with damp eyes,

Heavy regrets for loss dispositions,

Foolish flights encouraged by wrath,

Wild words let loose as straw dogs.

Anger is yet as a passing storm,

A season of mind dissipated by time,

By the rising of springs sunlight,

A morning's mist of regret suspended on the dawn.

PAUL WHITE

WOUNDS OF PRAYER

It is easy you know, to stumble and fall,

I do it all the time.

I try to look ahead, to see where I am going

And that is when

I trip over the uneven flagstones on life's footpath.

I squint with scrunched up eyes, trying to see past the dim streetlights

as they cast their mocking light in shallow pools of mournful promise,

Allowing the darkness of regret to spread its tentacles into the long hours of dis-remember recollections and rip them from my soul.

I stumble and I fall,

Knees scrapped and scared with past wounds of prayer,

Hands bloodied and blistered by the constant toil of resentful labour.

Chilled by the bitter winds of heartless indifference,

My bones rattle under the ashen parchment which drapes my body,

A loose cloak of shrivelled flesh.

I try to look ahead, to see where I am going

But my eyes are dimmed, misty cataracts of unfulfilled covenants,

My blindness shelters much, but cannot shield the screams

of aggravated exasperation which constantly falls upon me,

A constant drizzle of hindrance and obstruction pours from leaden skies of despondent defeat.

It is easy you know, to stumble and fall,

I do it all the time.

DARK WORDS

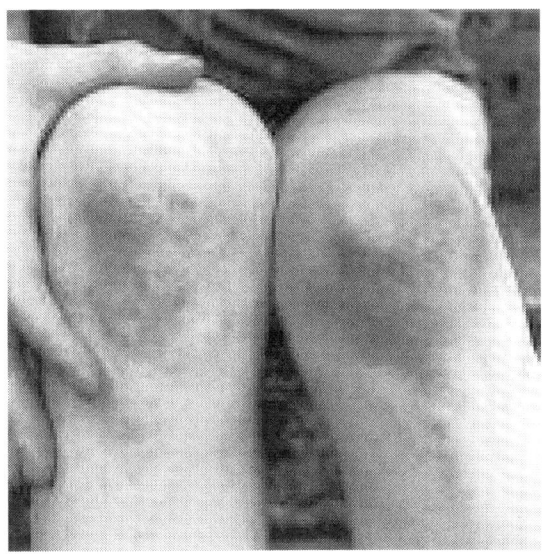

PAUL WHITE

CLOUDS

So, I jumped.

I say jumped, but it was more of a small hop or a large step.

The result was the same.

No matter how solid the clouds may look from above, especially when the sun is shining brightly, lighting them in a way they look like giant balls of cotton wool. They are in fact not solid.

Although clouds do have substance. A damp fog like quality, cold and scented like a dewy morning; like a dewy morning as the suns light is creeping over the horizon, when you wait in anticipation for the first glimpse of the fiery globe to expose its rays to your eyes.

As I fell, I realised how cold it was up here, how cold the air at two thousand five hundred feet feels, especially as my speed increased towards terminal velocity.

I knew I was going to die.

That was now an inevitability.

Something I could no longer change, even if I wanted to.

This is the strange thing; I accepted the fact without fear, without trepidation.

You see, as I plummeted earthwards I knew death was going to be the outcome all along. It was my choice, my decision to step out of the aeroplane.

Many times before, when I have flown as a passenger on business, or jetting off on holiday, I have looked out of the small port-hole type window and marvelled at the clouds.

How magnificent they look spread across the skies, shining bright white, pure white, reflecting the sunlight. How firm and sturdy they look.

I often imagined I could take a stroll across their mass; walk upon those billowing cushions of ethereal softness. Although I knew, of course, it would be impossible to do so in reality.

Today I am proving that fact.

I leave the clouds behind, way above me now as it happens and continue my ferocious decent towards terra firma, I have time to think about my life, my family and more. Running various scenarios through my mind of what they will do after my death.

Will my widow weep?

I think not.

Not until she has untangled her limbs for her lover.

Not until her presence in public demands her grieving; a façade of black veils smothering her crocodile tears, cloaking her joy of newly gained liberty from the confines of discarded vows.

I can hear the condolences spilling from the sour mouths of the attendees. Crooked and crumbling teeth surrounding insincere sentences spewed forth with emotionless intent.

I wonder briefly, who shall read the eulogy at my funeral service, how might they describe me?

Will they say I was a good man, kind, gentle hearted? One who loved life and family?

What lies shall they tell to placate the congregation, to adhere to convention?

Who was I kidding… a congregation, for me? I would be lucky if anyone showed at all, which is partly why I am here now, falling.

I can see the ground, it is as if it is rushing towards me and not vice versa.

It is also far warmer this low than above the clouds. Something which I find a strange ambiguity; as above the sun is brightly shining, here it is darker and grey. One of life's ironies no doubt?

Above the clouds, I could smell the earth. I do not mean the ground alone, but the earth itself, the ozone, the wind, the moisture. A rich wholesome scent which enlivens the senses, that stimulates the primal factors of the soul.

But here, so low, I can only smell mankind.

Metallic overtones carried on a bitter background of plasticised existence, a contaminated society riddled with the fumes of decaying morals and hatred.

All considered, I am not leaving very much of anything which holds true value behind me, am I?

These are my thoughts as I plummet downwards.

I hope the impact with the ground is quick, so I shall feel no pain.

I close my eyes, for these last few feet...

PAUL WHITE

DARK WORDS

ENTRY DENIED

You do not see me.

For I refuse you gaze,

Your stare,

Your scan.

You look at me.

And see my face,

My body,

My eyes.

But you do not see me.

Because I deny you,

Reject you,

Forbid you.

PAUL WHITE

You have hurt me.

Caused me harm,

Tormented me,

Brutalised my essence.

You do not see me.

I refuse you entry

To my soul,

To my being.

You look at me.

But all you see

Is my surface,

My shuttered self.

You can no longer see

Into my core,

Into my heart,

That bleeds with sorrow.

DARK WORDS

You shall never see

My pain,

My grief,

My sorrow.

All you shall see

Is a façade,

My wall,

My rejection of you.

YOUR ENTRY IS DENIED

PAUL WHITE

FRACTURED IMAGE

I know me, don't I?

I know who I am.

I am that calm collected person,

Always happy, smiling;

Content with my life, and

The world that surrounds me.

You know me, don't you?

I'm the one with the happy laugh.

Giggling along with you.

Chuckling to myself,

At my misfortunate acts.

Always laughing out loudly.

They know me, don't they?

Ask any of them.

They will say he is busy,

Hard working and industrious,

Consciences and reliable,

A nice person.

I see me. Don't I?

When I look into that mirror,

I see my fractured face staring back.

Shards of past life, of lost living,

Of pleasures faded into oblivion,

Waiting for welcome death.

I know me.

The true me. The inside me.

Marking time, waiting.

Acting out my role on the stage of life,

Getting by, dragging my soul through each day

I know. I see the true me,

Dying from the inside.

PAUL WHITE

LIGHTS OUT

Darkened room, blinds drawn.

Quiet, alone,

Faint Breath,

Muted heartbeat.

Absorbed, contemplative.

Sad, melancholy,

Woeful, dark

Despondent mood.

Depressed soul, desolate mind.

Thoughts, feelings,

Reflections, Contemplations

Darkened room, colt 45

PAUL WHITE

THE PEBBLE BANK

A slight mist hovered above the still waters all morning before it disappeared like a wisp. It returned as the sun touched the tops of the tallest trees cresting the far mountains, on its way down from the deepest azure blue sky I had witnessed in an age.

My husband and two sons are out on the lake, they have been all afternoon, swimming, fishing and fooling around. Occasionally the air carries a sound or a disjointed word to my ears. Often it is no more than a partial syllable, or a peel of laughter.
I look up, amazed at how far the sound of their voices travels.

The small blue and white boat, the craft my husband David named 'Samantha', after me, is only a tiny dot against the backdrop of trees and mountains, which reflect from the mirror calm waters. Only a shimmer, the slightest distortion, belies its fluidity.

My Grandfather built this cabin before I was born. The stumps of the trees he felled now long rotted into the lush greenness of the undergrowth. An undergrowth which has grown over the old tracks; the tracks he drove the horses and mules along as they carried the building materials and then his housewares to this point, to the lakeside.

There are no roads here. Once you drive as far as any wheeled vehicle can, you must then walk, or ride a horse if you have one. It is a mile or so, maybe a little more, climbing slowly for most of the distance along uneven, rocky footpaths which are seldom used.

Yet the view from the ridge is worth the trek alone. It is picture-postcard breathtakingly beautiful.

A tree-lined mountain valley with a crystal water lake. The brightest blue, whites and greens, interspersed with a riot of colourful wildflowers. From here, on the ridge, you can just see the log cabin nestling alongside the lake. It sits in this landscape perfectly, inviting, welcoming, tranquil.

I cannot recall one summer when I did not visit here. My earliest memories, I think I may have been five, possibly four? are of my Mother breastfeeding a baby. I think the child is my brother Kevin, but I do not know for sure.

Mother is sitting on the porch, in the rocking chair. I am at her feet looking up. That is it. That is my recollection. I know it is here, at the cabin. I cannot see it in my mind's eye, the detail has long faded, but it is a memory from the cabin. I know it with absolute certainty.

Another, not so fond memory, is one of me standing where I am now, on the smooth round pebbles of the shore. I am not confident shore is the correct term. Perhaps I should call it the pebble bank, I think that is a more accurate description. Anyway. I am standing here, my Father is trying to get me to wade deeper into the lake, to go swimming, but I refuse to go any further. I can feel the coldness of the water as it rises to mid-way up my thighs.

It is enough. Irrational fear washes over me, through me. My heart pounds. I am icy, yet beads of sweat spring onto my forehead. I feel a dizzying sickness. I turn and run up the bank, away from the edge of the lake. It was not just the water which scared me, there was more. Something beyond sinister which wrapped its icy talons of death around my heart that day. Portent, foreboding. An omen, who knows? I still shiver when I think of it.

My Father shouts and comes chasing after me. I hear Kevin calling. Looking back over my shoulder he is swimming and waving. My Father turns and runs into the lake, splashing his way to Kevin before picking him up and dunking him, head first, under the water. I said nothing of my fears, of the inward, silent screams as my own voice echoed in my own head. I had no wish to spoil the family's enjoyment of the summer. I know these were happy times. My ears were filled with laughter each and every day.

Now, I am sitting on a small cushion of a red candlewick. It is part of a re-cycled bedspread. Grandmother was a frugal soul. "Waste-not, want-not" "A stitch-in-time saves nine." I hear her voice echoing within.

The cushion is to soften the effect of the pebbles on my... my nether regions.

The pebbles here may have been worn smooth and round by the effect of ancient glaciers and the constant washing of lake water, but sitting upon them for any length of time without some form of protection becomes most uncomfortable indeed.

Hence the use of my Grandmothers candlewick cushion.

The boat is nearer now. I think it is heading this way, it is hard to tell. Sounds echo from the mountains. The mist has set again, once more a thin line hovering about a foot above the lake. It is crystal clear below and above this ribbon of mist. I sketch away furiously with pencils and charcoal, trying to capture this phenomenon on cartridge paper. Later, I hope to use these drawings to help me paint the moment, to capture this surreal effect, in oils.

The boat is getting closer. I can hear the faint drum of the engine.

I am pleased they are returning, yet disappointed the noise of boat is out of harmony with the rest of my surroundings. The regular hum of the small outboard motor is at odds with the breeze and the birdsong. It disturbs the balance in a way the weathered log cabin, even with a pale plume of bluish smoke rising from the chimney, does not.

The engine noise dies. Tranquillity returns. I suspect the boys are going for the last swim or shall try to catch one more fish, before returning. I lower my head and start sketching away. Soon the light will change, the afternoon will become early evening and this atmosphere, the very moment I am trying to capture, will have gone.

Nearer now, their voices are louder. Still jumbled, but louder. I smudge the charcoal, brushing it lightly, blowing the dust from the paper, trying to create depth without form.

Shouting, the boys are shouting. Clearly fooling about, showing off, seeking my attention. The sound of their calls makes me smile. I can feel my lips stretching. I cannot look up, not yet. I need two, three more strokes. I need to get this final moment onto paper.

David, my husband, has a deep voice that carries across crowded shops and busy restaurants. Often, I must hush him, ask him to talk softly. Somehow, he seems oblivious to his loudness and the disdainful look of other people. Now, his voice is coming across the lake as loud and as clear as ever. He is calling my name.

I slide the charcoal stick back into its tin, close the lid, fold the sketchbook closed and place both on the ground beside me before raising my head to look at the boys.
David is waving. I can see him and Peter, I think its Peter... or Phillip... it is hard to see from this distance. The light is fading, the mist thickening.

It is wrong, all wrong. They should be ashore now. The boat should be tied to the wooden jetty, not upturned, not sinking.

David dives under the water; I can just make out his feet kicking as he dives. The other head I can see; I am sure it is Peter. I should be able to tell my sons apart, to know how they look, even when wet, even at this distance. I scream out, calling their names, waving frantically from the pebbles.

I wade into the lake until I can feel the coldness of the waters mid-way up my thighs. It is as far as I can go. Irrational fear washes over me, through me. My heart pounds. I am icy, yet beads of sweat spring onto my forehead.
I feel a dizzying sickness.
I cannot help myself, I turn and run up the bank, away from the edge of the lake.

I recall that day, the day with my Father, with Kevin. This was what I felt when the icy cold waters touched my thighs, this was what I was experiencing. It was a premonition of today, of now, of death.

Looking behind me, over my shoulder I see the boat has gone, sunk under the calm waters of the lake. One small head... I think it is Peter, bobbing in the lake. He is swimming towards the shore, towards me.

There is no phone here. No signal. No Internet. The cabin is off-grid, isolated, tranquil even; unless you have a crisis unless your entire family are dying in front of your eyes. Then tranquil is not a nice word. It becomes mean, horrific, evil.

I grab a blanket, a flashlight and run back to the lake, back towards where Peter will come ashore. But there is no Peter. No head bobbing in the lake. There is no Peter, no Phillip, no David, no boat.

All looks calm, peaceful…tranquil.

It is as if they never existed. There is only a thin ribbon of mist floating a foot above the waters and the sound of the lake lapping at the pebble bank.

PAUL WHITE

MY SPECIAL PLACE

The place where you cannot be, the place you cannot even see.

This is the place you cannot find because it is within my mind,

Dark shades of hollow light, lost time that's taken flight.

Where fantasy is really fact and reality is your life hacked;

Your lies are now the naked truth, sold off cheap in a whorehouse booth,

And pirates pull your legs apart, to reach inside and grip your heart,

Where love is not a golden glow, but a pile of rubble, on skid row,

And laughing clowns smile with rotted teeth, while dirty hands fumble beneath,

All your wants, all your dreams, drown in bloody bathtubs, hear their screams,

Slashed with knives and cut with saws, skeletons give a round of applause.

Death becomes immortal life and Beelzebub your gender change wife.

Where sex comes only clamped in chains, whip your arse with bamboo canes,

Crawl to me over the floor, on your knees, like a submissive whore.

Life and light are just shades of grey, where nuns have forgotten how to pray,

And crosses hold the dying up high, screaming in pain at the sullen sky,

Upon the breeze, breath of carrion crow, pass dreams of hope, row on row,

Despair and anger and grief and gloom reflect down from a rancid moon.

This is the place you cannot find because it lives within my mind,

And if I let you take a peek, forevermore your soul you shall seek.

PAUL WHITE

SIX WEEKS

They tell me my name is David.

I am thirteen years old.

At this moment, I am standing in a doorway, looking into a room.

There are no windows. The only light emits from a single lamp, a bare bulb hanging from a thin yellowing cable in the centre of the ceiling.

In one corner of the room is a rectangular raised area; six feet long, three feet wide and about four inches high. In another corner is a plain wooden chair, the sort once used in classrooms. The third corner holds a cracked white hand basin with a single tap, a cold-water tap.

That is the total of the furnishings.

I hate this room; although I have an affinity for it.

I am not sure what I am feeling; loathing, sadness, fear, relief, a vile longing? All these emotions are flowing within me, through me, in waves.

My body is trembling. I cannot stop it.

One part of me wants to enter, to walk into the room, to sit on the chair or on the raised area and look about from the inside.

But I am frozen to this spot. My legs refuse to move. An invisible barrier prevents me entering.

A tear drips from my eye and runs down my cheek. I wipe it away with the back of my hand. Snort back the mucus in my nose. I am breathing heavily, long breaths sighs. In, out. I fight the urge to cry, blinking to stop tears from escaping.

It is the first time I have visited this room for six weeks. Six weeks.

That may not seem a long time to you. But for me it is a lifetime; more than a lifetime.

Six weeks is the only period of my entire life I have not been enclosed by the four walls which make this room.

I cannot recall life before, if it actually existed.

If I existed.

Everything I knew changed the day the door, the one where I now stand, came crashing inwards, flying open as the men came rushing in.

It is all a bit of a blur. They were dressed in black, shouting, screaming and banging, waving their guns before them, torches shining into my eyes.

I do not remember too much, except the fear. The way my heart jumped. The icy coldness which swept through my body and my screaming.

I can still hear that.

The high-pitched screech which came from somewhere inside of me, which hurt my ears as it vibrated from these bare walls.

It was an inhuman sound, so shrill I scared myself further.

It is what I hear now, my own fear echoing around this room. Although all is, in truth, deadly silent now.

I think it has been this way since they took me. Rescued me, they say.

Six weeks ago.

They tell me I am thirteen years old and my name is David.

Although, I do not know what those things mean.

LEAVING HERE

I am hitch-hiking. Thumb out, smiling.

Hoping the next approaching car or truck will be the one which stops and picks me up.

It is a lost art these days, hitchhiking.

I blame the media. Mind you, I blame the media for most things nowadays.

Hold your arm out straight, thumb erect, look at the driver directly. Look into his or her eyes. The trick is not to look threatening, smile sweetly, but not like a demonic axe murderer, even if you are one.

It is a numbers game. Sooner or later someone will stop.

Then it is your choice. Take the ride or not?

Your judgement, you choose.

Life is like thumbing a lift. You stick your arm out and watch who passes you by.

You see who stops, who you attract.

Then it is your choice. Take the ride or not.

Much depends on where they are going and how far. Much depends on where you are going and in which direction. Sometimes it works out, sometimes you get stranded.

Of course, you can always find yourself in a bad place. The wrong ride. The wrong situation. The wrong time; or even all three.

That is life or death. Yours or theirs.

It is your choice, or maybe it is theirs, now?

This is my choice, hitchhiking.

Waiting for that random stop. The moment which shall see the merging of two unconnected lives. The creation of the butterfly effect on our separate, soon to be connected, destinies.

What instances can alter the future? My future, theirs, yours?

My future just now is to go from here to somewhere else. I have no concern as to where I may find somewhere else; just as long as it is far away from where I now am.

You see, here is not just a physical location, here is where my life has taken me and it is not a place I am fond of.

So, I am leaving, or running away, if you prefer to call it that.

I am good at running. Or maybe I simply think I am.

I have done a lot of running recently and I always seem to end up back here. Back with me, with this life.

So, maybe I am not so good at running after all.

Maybe I should consider, rather than running away I am simply on a journey, an accidental, impromptu journey, of which I have little true control. A voyage of discovery, steered by the vagaries of life's arbitrary and indiscriminate influences.

Possibly the car which stops, the driver who deems it considerate to pick up a hitchhiker, is all part of a greater plan; the impending encounter between us, pre-ordained.

Or possibly it will just be a totally random happenchance.

I think the latter.

Firstly, because I do not believe in predestined fate and secondly, I like the word happenchance; it rolls off the tongue easily and with much joviality.

All considered, the one thing which is still undisclosed is my destination. When shall I stop running, where shall my journey end.

I do not suggest my final destination. I know what that is. I know someday the grim reaper will swing his scythe and harvest my soul.

Beyond which, I await enlightenment.

I simply refer to a point when I shall find some true purpose, or even some vague significance, of my rather futile existence.

Shall I there meet the love of my life? Will such time hold the key to my freedom, unlock an unfounded conviction of certainty and release my doubts and fears, allowing them to flee into infinity?

Or shall I find another veracity?

Maybe I will encounter a sudden epiphany, a conscious comprehension of the meaning of life and the universe.

Or not.

A small blue car slows in answer to my raised thumb. It pulls over to the side of the road. I run up to the window and bend low to speak with the driver.

'I'm going south' she says.

'So am I' I replied. South seemed to be as good a direction as any other.

'Jump in' she says, patting the passenger seat.

Am I running or am I travelling?

Shall I ever return?

This is now my choice.

Take the ride… or not.

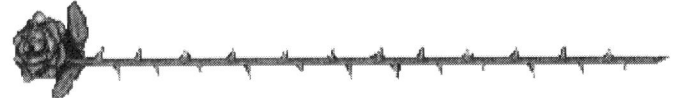

OVERLOAD

A thousand garbled voices echo from the tower,

Distorted words reverberate, yearning for Narcissus.

Mangled incantations invoked collectively,

Babel reigns supreme, throbbing tympanic membrane.

I am only one, I call out.

My voice unheard.

Cacophony is king, sovereign over silence.

Now pulsating temporal lobes,

Pounding all thought to blacked particles.

I scream out, screech my lungs dry.

Still, the voices persist, constant intensity,

Stabbing into my head, sharp needles piercing my mind.

I pray for quiet.

Whisper, a murmur of breath whisked away,

Smothered by a thousand garbled voices,

Take me from this Barbican,

Let me walk in voiceless air

Hush now.

Let me be.

ROLL OF THE DICE

The Bar

This bar was like one of so many bars located on a deteriorating city street. The type of bar which exist only because the last few regular customers have not yet passed away.

Even the exterior slouched wearily, like an aged man with asthma, over the grey pavement. The interior fared little better. It was painted in a sad shade of shit brown, covered with a dandruff of dust.

The only glimmer of promise reflected from the whisky bottles standing in disorderly conduct on the grimy shelves and from the brass beer pump which looked incongruous standing erect in the centre of the counter like a golden penis.

The true irony was the beer pump alone was the only object in the entire bar that could stand proudly upright. Its very presence, so predominantly on display, seemed to mock the old men whose only recollection of penile function is shrouded in the befuddled fog of distant memory.
I am one of those men.

For the last twenty years, I have parked my sallow arse on the bar stool at the far end of the counter. It was for me, the primary position of the entire bar. From this perch, I could observe all the activities of the inhabitants. much as a vulture seeking deceased carcasses.

The scuffed oxblood-red leather seat of my bar stool has, over the years, taken on the imprint of my backside, so now I simply aligned my crack with the ridge of the seat and slot myself into it, rather than sit upon it.

The counter was worn, light patches revealed themselves from beneath fake mahogany stain, places where my arms constantly rested and from the perpetual placement of whisky tumblers and beer bottles.

This is my world.

It is a world where my drinking partners were as familiar as the odour of stale sweat from my armpits. Neither of which are attractive or welcome, but both constant in their companionship.

The Bartender.

Jefferson was the bartender, he was also the proprietor. His wrinkled complexion was as pale and insipid as the warm beer he served.

Years ago, before the factories closed and the welfare checks arrived, Jefferson had a wife and daughter who assisted in the bar.

It was no secret Jefferson's wife, Sally played around a bit. In fact, Sally had affairs with half of the menfolk in the town and one-night stands with the other half.

Sally left Jefferson once the town began to die and the men moved away.
Some say Sally quit the bar to be with a lumberjack from Arkansas.

Others say Jefferson finally had enough of Sally's slutish ways and kicked her butt out.

But the guy's in here, in the bar, allege Jefferson killed the bitch. The rumour is, Jefferson, chopped Sally into chunks in the cellar below, before driving out to the swamps and hand feeding her, piece by piece to the alligators.

As for Mary, Jefferson's daughter, well she hung around town for a while after Sally left, but following speculation Jefferson was getting from his own daughter that which he never got from his wife, she too upped sticks.

Small towns can spread some evil rumours.

Once, three years ago, Mary came back to visit.

It was a Sunday.

Mary was sporting two children. Twins, one boy and one girl.

The kids were as black as the ace of spades and so was Mary's husband.

They did not stay for long. Not even long enough to attend chapel.

Mary never returned since that Sunday.

Jefferson was not best pleased by Mary's presence in the bar or the town.

Jefferson hated black folk.

In fact, Jefferson hated anybody who was not white and from this state.

Even those who were, Jefferson only tolerated.

The fact is, Jefferson was not a people person.

This is why, I guess, Jefferson turned out to be such stony-faced sourpuss, a miserable bastard.

I cannot recall seeing Jefferson smile, not once, not ever.

The Whore.

Dianne staggered over and sat on the stool next to mine. I did my best to ignore her, slightly turning away from her. But as she pulled the zipper of my trouser flies down, I had to acknowledge her presence.

I pushed her hand away.
There are three main reasons I did so.

The first is, it felt dirty to have this haggard whore fondling my groin in a public place, particularly so early in the evening when most people were only half drunk.

Secondly, I had drunk so much whisky over the proceeding decade I could no longer get it up, at least not without an awful lot of stimulation, and that was on a good day.
This was not a good day.

Although this condition was true for most of the patrons in this least salubrious of establishments, I was not prepared to publicly exhibit my dysfunction or expose myself to ridicule.

Thirdly, I was not prepared to pay Dianne for what she would give me for free later tonight if I asked nicely and plied her with cheap drinks.

Dianne had been frequenting this bar for a whole lot longer than I. It has been said, in the bar's heyday she was the town's best and wealthiest hooker.

Some say she was quite a pretty young thing back then, but passing time and the countless poundings from a million stiff cocks had clearly taken their toll on Dianne's looks.

Nowadays Dianne thickly coated her face with powder and painted her lips bright red.

She did not do this to attract men, it was so she would not recognise herself in the mirror, not see how decayed her skin and furrowed her face had become.

Dianne hates herself.

You can see it when you look into her eyes. They are empty of emotion, cold and distant hollows of unfulfilled childhood dreams, whetted by screams of violent abuse and self-loathing.

I dislike Dianne with a passion, yet I have used her body, as have most of the men and some of the women who are in this bar tonight.

Sometimes you become so lonely, so depressed, you will seek any form of comfort, however fruitless you know it to be.

For those few short hours, you can pretend your life is better, even pretend you have a life.

Although it is only a transient, it can for that short moment of time dull the pain of your futile existence.

The Irishman

Sean was out of prison, once again.

There was a time, many times in fact when Sean was released from wherever he had been incarcerated, he would celebrate his freedom in this bar with a whole host of well-wishers.

They would drink hard in the way only the Irish can do. They would talk louder than each other, play a style of music called a jig on instruments they brought along, dance like whirling dervishes until the sun began creeping over the rooftops and end the party by shouting and brawling in the street.

They were good times.

But this night, Sean is seated in a dank corner of the bar, which smelled of stale urine and cigarette ash.

Tonight, the only music was the tinny sounds coming from the badly tuned transistor radio located behind the bar and from the regular beat of the occasional passing goods train, shipping the last hopes of prospect into the darkness of the night.

Sean was alone. He was seventy-four years old, thirty-two of which he wasted, imprisoned behind bars.

Years ago, Sean had been a New York Police Officer. It was way back when the man on the beat ruled the streets. Whatever was going down on Sean's beat, cash was going into Sean's pocket.

But times change. although some people do not.
Sean did not.

After his discharge from the force, Sean turned to professional crime. Only he was not a professional criminal.

Sean boasted he would make himself rich, fast. But all Sean achieved over the years was to lose everything he had. First, he lost his wife and children and then his home, followed by his freedom and his liberty.

The only constant in Sean's life is this bar, yet even here he has no friends.

All the old well-wishers and hangers-on faded away, some were still locked up, others got out of town, some had died.

A few managed to do all three.

The only possible gain for Sean was finding God between the grey bars and stone walls of the correctional facilities where he spent most of his adult life.

Why God should wish to live in such a place is beyond me.

If I were a gambling man, I would bet it will not be St. Peter who greets Sean at the pearly gates, but Satan, who will lead Sean down below, to the fiery pit of eternal damnation.

Sean knows death shall shortly be knocking on his door. In fact, if you listen carefully, you can hear the reaper calling his name.

Me

So why am I here? Why am I in this bar?

Do you want the existential answer or the truth?

The truth is simple.

You see the Devil made a pact with God regarding love, the real long-term committed relationship type of love. True, time-tested, honest love.

God and the Devil sit together each day, they throw a pair of dice to decide the fate of couples in these loving types of relationships.

When it is your time, they cast the die to see your destiny.

A double six means death, your death. Guess what, that is the lucky number.

If your partner gets a double-one, they will die; which means it is the unlucky number, for you.

I would wish for a double six.

In fact, if I were you, I would pray for a double six.

Why?

Well, for the past twenty years, the same time as I have been visiting this bar, I have been alone.

My wife got a double-one.

Snake eyes.

So, they took her from me. Left me here to grieve, alone.

I was walking back from the cemetery when I first came into this bar for a beer, just one or two, to drown my sorrows.

Sitting here, right here on this very stool for the first time, the fact I was alone hit me like a sledgehammer.
When I say alone, I do not mean I was simply on my own, but I was alone.
Utterly alone.

Regardless of how many people were here, how many people were with me, I was alone.
Period.

I have come here every day since, to drink and to forget.
But I cannot forget.
So, I drink to dull the pain.
But the hurt is always there, lingering, clinging to my heart with its sharp piercing talons of despair.

I have tried many times to join my wife. But I am refused death. It is not my time yet.
They will not roll the dice for me.

So, I sit here and wait and carry on drinking.

I carry my wife's picture in my wallet, her memory in my head and her love in my heart.

Still, my soul longs to be reunited with hers.

Until my time, until the dice fall in my favour, I shall sit on the worn, cracked leather of this stool surveying the brown forget-ness of the disregarded patrons of this bar. I accept my lot as a surveyor of gilded phallic representation, of soiled glass and peeling veneers, for it is these which reflect the dull light, or the little that is left, of the essence of my spirit and the consciousness of my being.

I shall cherish death when it arrives. I will welcome it with open arms.

"Come now" I shall call to out to Charon, "Ferry me across Acheron, for I am ready, I wish to enter the underworld".

PAUL WHITE

DARK WORDS

THE SUITCASE

The suitcase is here, in the hall, waiting for me.

Waiting for me to pick it up and walk out.

Walk out of the door and into the future.

My future, my unknown and uncertain future.

Time and words, and no words, and grunts,

Sounds and glances and gestures of the hands.

These were said, done, unconsidered.

Without realisation. Without thought.

You were near me, yet so far.

We were together, but apart.

Drifting on a sea of comfortable indifference,

Blown by the winds of unappreciated availability.

Too soon our voices lost in the fogs of common devaluation;
The lighthouse of couple, of togetherness, of being one,
Dimmed in the darkness of uncaring attitudes.
The storms of tomorrow rising unseen beyond the horizon of honest care.

Lying next to you, the distance is greater than when
We share the table and break bread.
Eyes willing words, but minds playing truant
Wandering aimlessly into the fields of what if's and maybe's.

Dreams of how things should be,
Of promises abandoned in the forests of repetition.
Past wants and longings, now heavy burdens,
Dragging broken hearts earthwards, depressing hope.

To have looked up, looked into her eyes,

To have smiled on occasion.

Spoken softly, those almost forgotten words, once more

into her ears and

Said loudly with all the others I have held within.

Kissed foreheads and cheeks and lips

And the nape of her neck.

Held her close as never to let her loose, as my arms

once did back then,

Back in the beginning, when I listened more to the

meaning of her words.

I heft the suitcase. Juggle its weight.

It settles into my hand, balanced. Like an old friend.

An old friend I have no wish to see again.

I nod silently to my foolish self.

My silence was not for her,

Those unsaid words bursting inside of me, full of meaning.

The gestures were not expressions of attitude, never taken for granted,

But of my own fear, my acknowledgement of inadequate self.

I know I am far, far less than she deserves. Far, far less than she can have.

I slide further into the depressions of apprehension and self-loathing,

Dragging her with me, day by day, pulling her into my gloom.

Her light fading, dulled by my smothering failings,

would be only twilight of unfulfilled potent

Glancing back, I catch her shadow by the doorway, as she withdraws into the room

Ethereal, shadowy, fleeting from my eyes.

She will not watch me leave, her ears waiting only for sound of the door to close,
Eyes blinded by salty tears and trails of mascara on her pale cheeks, supported by sore throat.

I do not blame her. Nothing to see here. Move along, please.
Yet still, I stall. Half turn, prolonging abandoned hope, longing for what never was
For what never could be, not truly, not ever; even given time anew.
I am wrong. So very wrong. For her, for me. For what was never to be us.

I pull the heavy wooden door closed; firmly sealing the past, all previous moments now history.
Turning, I see life stretched out before me. Stretched out on the uncertain highway of unimaginable possibility.

Inside another life is drying her eyes, sniffing back anger of wasted years, swilling the final drops of Merlot from the glass.

The past is gone, the future beckons, like that glass. Awaiting the opening of a new bottle.

My suitcase is full. I have no room to carry regrets into tomorrow.

My features etched and forged from the scars of memory.

Beliefs bony hand points onwards, the direction I shall follow to my destiny.

Hope alone walks with me, lighting my path, casting aside my inner fear.

JACK OF HEARTS

Life Depends on which cards land because the Devils made the deal.
To be the King or the Queen of Hearts is what you wish to feel.
So, pick them up, fan them out, take a look and see,
There's the Black Jack of Clubs, his grinning back with glee.

Sitting behind him is the Ace of Spades, now that's your bad luck
Just like the hand that life dealt you, it doesn't give a flying fuck.

Now, the King and Queen will only be in your nightly dreams
And that heart you so desire is further away than it seems.

"I'll raise you ten," he says, with an evil sneer
You want to tear his face off, rip it from ear to ear,
Your last silver dollar hits the table, landing in the pot
That's it, your all up, it's the very last you've got.

Just one slender chance, you willingly embrace,
Because nothing now can fill, what is an empty space
And that nothing will leave you just about level;
Until you sell your vacant soul, to Beelzebub the Devil.

You lose again, just like every fucking day,
Just get up from the table, it's time to walk away.
Tomorrow is Valentines, a day of true romance,
When lovers reveal their passions, hoping for a chance;

Where wine, champagne, chocolates and red flowers bloom,
When a thousand pairs of naked feet scuttle into hotel rooms,
Where the lost and lonely sit and weep in darkened empty homes,
And stare at the blank glass screens of their silent mobile phones.

Where all life's gambles lay in ruins, upon that flat green baize,
And those who lost wander the streets, in a lonesome daze.
When love is merely some recall, that is so hard to find,
Something fleeting, escaping the consciousness of mind,
Where the fallen Jack of Hearts lays upon the floor
With one arm raised, finger pointing, showing you the door.

PAUL WHITE

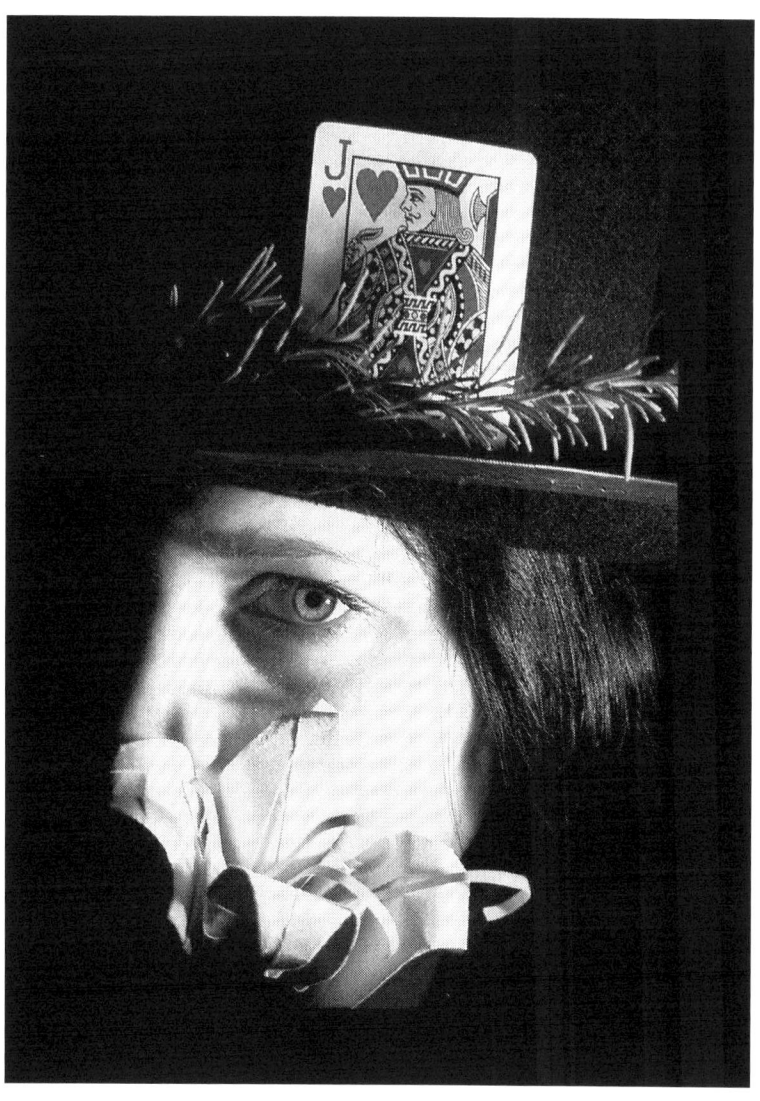

WHEN YOU GO

Take this knife to my throat,

Cut me deep and watch me choke.

Kiss my cheek and walk away.

I'll use my last breath to say,

I still love you.

PAUL WHITE

AFTERWORD

Thank you for reading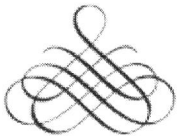

I hope you found the stories captivating, intriguing and thought-provoking... although not necessarily in that order.

You may like to read another of my short story collections, a series of three books called **'Tales of Crime & Violence.'**
Available as Volumes 1, 2 & 3, as paperbacks, or on Kindle.

Tales of Crimes & Violence looks deeper into the human psyche, the mind and spirits of those involved and asks questions.
Are they the perpetrators or the victims? The innocent caught in the crossfire or is there more to their presence than meets the eye? Maybe they are willing participants, or have they been forced or coerced into taking part?

*F*ancy something more a little more light-hearted?

Then **'The Abduction of Rupert DeVille'** is right up your street.

Rupert is a lost soul, a bumbling lad staggering through daily life when he meets Carla... In the morning, of the day he is to propose, Rupert is snatched off the street... and his adventures begin.

"The Abduction of Rupert DeVille is a book which transcends genre.
Like a great painting or a wonderfully composed piece of music, Paul White has managed to mix and blend the various disciplines of his art into one amazing novel.
Is 'The Abduction of Rupert DeVille' a suspense mystery, yes. But it is also a thriller, a romance of love, a humorous tome, a story of finding oneself and much more.

Whatever type book you regularly read, I suggest your next book be this one.

I had to keep turning the pages because this book made me cry. I had tears running down my cheeks, not only from the emotions which Paul portrays so well but also from the laughter caused by the most absurd situations which, on occasion, the characters find themselves involved.

Please, do not have any preconceptions about the Abduction of Rupert DeVille, just get yourself a copy and read it.

Five stars all round from me."

Andy Peterson.

ABOUT THE AUTHOR

Paul White is a prolific storyteller, a wordsmith,

tale weaver and an Amazon international bestselling author.

He writes from his Yorkshire home, near a quiet market town in the East Ridings.

Paul has published several books, from full-length novels to short story collections, poetry, children's books, semi-fiction, non-fiction & military social history. He also contributes to various collective anthologies.

You can find more about Paul, his current works-in-progress, artworks and other projects, by visiting his website:

http://paulznewpostbox.wix.com/paul-white

PAUL WHITE

BOOKS
Click on title for link

Fiction

The Abduction of Rupert DeVille
(Paperback & eBook)

Tales of Crime & Violence
(Volumes 1, 2 & 3)

Semi-Fiction

Life in the War Zone
(Paperback only)

Poetry

Teardrops & White Doves
(Paperback & Outsized Hardcover)

Shadows of Emotion
(Paperback & eBook)

Military Social History

HMS Tiger - Chronicles of the last big cat
(Outsized Hardcover only)

The Pussers Cook Book
(Hardcover version)
(Paperback & Hardcover)

Jack's Dits
(Paperback)

Children's stories

The Rabbit Joke
(Outsized Hardcover)

A Treasure chest of children's stories
(Anthology)

Music / Art

Iconic
(Hardcover)

Anthologies
(Joint Author / Contributor)

Awethors anthology – *Light volume*

Awethors December anthology – *Dark volume*

Individually Together
(Storybook publishing)

Violence, Control & other kinds of Love
(Abyssinian press)

Looking into the Abyss
(TOAD Publishing)

A Treasure chest of children's stories
(Plaisted publishing house)

Midsummer Anthology
(Jara publishing)

PAUL WHITE

Paul has also published several 'standalone' short, (*or not so short,*) stories as Electric Eclectic Novelettes

Three Floors Up

Miriam's Hex

North to Maynard

Mechanical Mike

Printed in Great Britain
by Amazon